Earth's Amazing Animals

Animal Superpowers
MASTERS of DISGUISE

Joanne Mattern

RED CHAIR PRESS

Animal Superpowers is produced and published by Red Chair Press:
Red Chair Press LLC   PO Box 333   South Egremont, MA 01258-0333
www.redchairpress.com

Publisher's Cataloging-In-Publication Data
Names: Mattern, Joanne, 1963-

Title: Masters of disguise / Joanne Mattern.

Other Titles: Core content library.

Description: South Egremont, MA : Red Chair Press, [2019] | Series: Earth's amazing animals : animal superpowers | Includes glossary, Power Word science term etymology, fact and trivia sidebars. | Includes bibliographical references and index. | Summary: "Shapes, colors, or markings. Some mammals, birds, and fish use unusual camouflage to hide in plain sight."--Provided by publisher.

Identifiers: LCCN 2018937237 | ISBN 9781634404211 (library hardcover) | ISBN 9781634404273 (ebook)

Subjects: LCSH: Animals--Juvenile literature. | Camouflage (Biology)--Juvenile literature. | CYAC: Animals. | Camouflage (Biology)

Classification: LCC QL751.5 .M382 2019 (print) | LCC QL751.5 (ebook) | DDC 591.47/2--dc23

Copyright © 2019 Red Chair Press LLC

RED CHAIR PRESS, the RED CHAIR and associated logos are registered trademarks of Red Chair Press LLC.

All rights reserved. No part of this book may be reproduced, stored in an information or retrieval system, or transmitted in any form by any means, electronic, mechanical including photocopying, recording, or otherwise without the prior written permission from the Publisher. For permissions, contact info@redchairpress.com

Illustrations by Tim Haggerty

Maps by Joe LeMonnier

Photo credits: iStock

Printed in United States of America

102018 1P CGBS19

Table of Contents

Introduction 4

Rainbow Disguise: The Chameleon 6

Blending In: The Pygmy Seahorse 10

Tree or Insect? Leaf and Stick Insects 14

Wanted Dead or Alive: The Opossum 18

A Feathery Disguise: The Owl 22

Spotted Danger: The Leopard 26

Animal Disguises 30

Glossary 31

Learn More in the Library 31

Index 32

Introduction

Sometimes fighting is the best way to get rid of an enemy. Other times it's enough to look big and scary. But often the best defense is not to be seen at all! The animal kingdom is full of animals that use **camouflage** to stay hidden. Other animals use camouflage so they can surprise animals they want to eat. Either way, staying hidden is a great way to stay alive.

Some animals take camouflage a step further. Like the superheroes in movies and stories, some animals have special tricks or special body parts that help them hide. Some superheroes and villains are masters of disguise. Let's take a look at some of the masters of disguise in the animal world.

Rainbow Disguise:
The Chameleon

When it comes to disguises, no animal is better at hiding than the chameleon. A chameleon is a lizard of many colors. It uses those colors to stay out of sight.

You might have seen a chameleon in a cartoon changing colors and patterns as it moves from one surface to another. Cartoons make changing look quick and easy. In the real world, chameleons change color slowly. And they can't become any pattern they want. However, they can still create some pretty colorful disguises.

Chameleons also use color to communicate.

Now You Know!

A chameleon's eyes can move independently from each other.

Now You Know!

A chameleon's sticky tongue is longer than its body.

Here's how a chameleon's disguise works. This **reptile** has four layers of skin. The top layer protects the chameleon's body. The second layer has red and yellow **pigments**. The third layer has a dark pigment. The fourth layer can reflect white. As a chameleon moves from one color to another, its skin cells get bigger or smaller. This allows different pigments to become stronger. That changes the animal's color.

Why would a chameleon want to change color? Changing color helps the chameleon stay out of sight. So when an insect flies by, it has no idea that the chameleon is sitting there, ready to snap it up and eat it!

Gotcha!

Blending In: The Pygmy Seahorse

It's easy to see how the seahorse got its name. This creature lives in the oceans, and the shape of its body does make it look like a horse. However, seahorses are fish. And they can do some things no other fish can do.

The pygmy seahorse is one of the smallest seahorses. It measures less than an inch (2.5 cm) long. Its small size isn't the only thing about the pygmy seahorse that makes it hard to see. This seahorse can also change color to blend in with the world around it. Just like the chameleon, seahorses have different pigments in their skin. These pigments change depending on what surrounds the animal.

This pygmy seahorse blends in with red coral.

Now You Know!
Pygmy seahorses can swim very fast.

Pygmy seahorses live in and around coral. Corals are usually bright in color. The pygmy seahorse is too! When a pygmy seahorse floats next to a patch of coral, its color and shape make it disappear. Pygmy seahorses hide so well that scientists didn't even know about them. One day a scientist was studying some coral, and a seahorse popped out! *What a surprise!*

Seahorses eat tiny animals called **plankton**. They suck in the plankton and swallow them whole. Seahorses eat this way because they do not have any teeth.

Now You Know!

Female seahorses lay eggs. But the male carries the eggs in a pouch on its body until they hatch.

Leaf insects blend in among leaves.

Now You Know!
Some people keep leaf and stick insects as pets.

Tree or Insect?
Leaf and Stick Insects

Sometimes an animal's color helps it hide. Other times, the shape of the animal's body does the job. For leaf and stick insects, both color and shape create their disguises!

Leaf insects and stick insects are part of a family called Phasmids. Stick insects are long and thin, just like sticks! These insects are usually brown in color. When a stick insect stands still, it looks just like a brown twig on a branch.

Most leaf insects are wide and green. Like their name says, they look like leaves. Some leaf insects have yellow or brown patches. These colors help them blend in even better.

Both leaf insects and stick insects are **herbivores**. Like other insects, these creatures lay eggs. Since these insects look like plants, it's no surprise that their eggs look like seeds! The eggs lie under dead leaves or underground until they hatch. The young insects look like tiny adults.

Now You Know!

Stick insects can be up to 21 inches (a half-meter) long.

Wanted Dead or Alive:
The Opossum

Sometimes hiding isn't a good enough disguise. When that happens, some animals try something else. They pretend to be dead. The most well-known animal that does this is the opossum.

Opossums weigh about 15 pounds (7 kg). These animals are very peaceful. So, when an opossum is scared by a **predator** or another danger, it doesn't want to fight. Instead, it plays dead.

To play dead, the opossum falls down. Its body goes limp. Its feet curl into balls. An opossum can even let out a really stinky smell. The predator is fooled into thinking the opossum is truly dead. About 40 minutes later, the opossum wakes up and goes on its way.

Opossums often climb trees in daylight to stay safe.

Now You Know!

Opossums are the only marsupials that live in North America. All the others live in Australia or New Guinea.

Opossum playing dead

When they aren't playing dead, opossums spend their time hanging out in trees or looking for food. These animals are **omnivores**. They eat insects, eggs, frogs, fruit, and many other foods. They will also eat dead animals.

Power Word: Think of the word *devour* (duh-v'hour), it means <u>to eat</u>. *Omni* means <u>ALL things</u>. So, an omnivore eats both plant and animal foods.

Opossums give birth to about 14 babies at a time. When they are born, the babies are so tiny, they can all fit in a teaspoon. They crawl into a pouch on their mother's belly until they are bigger. When the babies are older, the mother opossum often carries them all on her back.

Now You Know!
Opossums are not bothered by the venom in snakes they eat.

Now You Know!

The snowy owl is white, not dark like other owls. Its white color helps disguise it in the snow.

A Feathery Disguise:
The Owl

It's hard to catch your dinner when your **prey** can see you. To solve this problem, many animals disguise themselves. The owl is one of these masters of disguise. This bird is so good at hiding, its prey probably never sees it coming until it's too late.

There are many different kinds of owls. Most owls are dark. This dark color helps them blend in with the trees. An owl often sits in a hole in a tree trunk. It is disguised as part of the bark and blends right in with the wood around it. An owl's brown and white coloring also helps it hide in dirt and rocks on the ground.

Owls are part of a group called birds of prey. Most owls are **carnivores**. They eat insects, mice, and other small animals. An owl is **nocturnal**. Its senses of sight and hearing are very strong. It can see and hear other animals before they know the owl is after them. Once an owl spots its prey, it flies down on wings that are so quiet, the prey never hears it coming.

Owl with prey

Owls swallow their prey whole. Later, they will pass a hard **pellet**. Inside the pellet are the bones and fur of the owl's prey.

Now You Know!

An owl can turn its head almost all the way around and can even see behind its body.

Great Horned Owl

Spotted Danger: The Leopard

You would think having spots would make an animal stand out. Actually, the opposite is true. Spots can help an animal be a master of disguise. This is true of the snow leopard, or panther.

But most leopards live where it is warm all year long. They hunt large animals, like deer and antelope. To catch its large prey, the leopard moves slowly through the tall grass. Its spots help it blend in. If its prey doesn't see the leopard coming, it won't be long before it becomes the leopard's lunch!

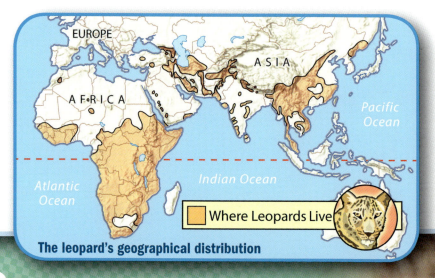

The leopard's geographical distribution

Now You Know!

Most leopards live where it's warm. But the snow leopard lives in the cold mountains of Central Asia.

Now You Know!

A leopard's spots are called rosettes because they are shaped like small roses.

Leopards are great tree climbers. These big, powerful cats sleep in the trees. They eat up there too. A leopard can't eat a large animal all at once. So, it drags the **carcass** up into the tree to eat later.

Some leopards are all black. These cats are usually called black panthers. Black leopards have black spots too. They are just hard to see against the black fur.

Animal Disguises

The animals in this book all have clever ways to stay out of sight. Sometimes animal disguises protect the animal from predators. Other times, the disguise helps a predator hide while it hunts its prey. And sometimes, a disguise is a way to fool other animals into leaving the creature alone. No matter what type of disguise an animal uses, it is a great way for the animal to survive.

It's fun to read about superheroes and their amazing powers of disguise. But even superheroes aren't as good as these animal masters of disguise!

Glossary

camouflage coloring that hides an animal

carcass the body of a dead animal

carnivores animals that eat other animals

herbivores animals that eat plants

marsupials mammals that carry their babies in pouches until they are fully developed

nocturnal active at night

omnivores animals that eat both plants and other animals

pellet a small mass of bones and feathers, passed from the stomach

pigments substances that create colors

plankton a tiny sea creature

predator an animal that hunts other animals for food

prey animals that are hunted by other animals for food

reptile an animal that is cold-blooded, has scaly skin, and lays eggs

Learn More in the Library

Johnson, Rebecca L. *Masters of Disguise: Amazing Animal Tricksters.* Millbrook Press, 2016.

Riehecky, Janet. *Camouflage and Mimicry: Animal Weapons and Defenses.* Capstone Press, 2012.

Snow Leopards
https://www.worldwildlife.org/species/snow-leopard

Index

camouflage 4
coral 12
lizard 6
marsupial 19
panther 26, 29
phasmids 15
pigments .9, 10

About the Author

Joanne Mattern is the author of nearly 350 books for children and teens. She began writing when she was a little girl and just never stopped! Joanne loves nonfiction because she enjoys bringing science topics to life and showing young readers that nonfiction is full of compelling stories! Joanne lives in the Hudson Valley of New York State with her husband, four children, and several pets!